BYE BYE ASHES

norine rae

Bye Bye Ashes

norine rae

Illustrator: Alice Hou Mengyao

Editor: Debbie Li Ying

Aflame International Ministries Publishing

ISBN: 0692307923
ISBN **9780692307922**

DEDICATION

It is with sincere love and devotion that I dedicate this work to my mom, Norma Doyel. Thank you mom for all you have taught me, but especially for loving me and showing me how to overcome difficulties in life with persistence, zeal, and determination. Truly you have been an inspiration for me.

Contents

Isaiah 61:3

*To grant those who mourn in Zion, Giving them a garland instead of ashes,
The oil of gladness instead of mourning, The mantle of praise instead of a
spirit of fainting. So they will be called oaks of righteousness, The planting of
the LORD, that He may be glorified.*

Chapter 1: The Dream

Once upon a time there was a lovely young girl named Jasmine. Jasmine spent much of her day thinking about how wonderful it would be if she could live in the magical kingdom just over the mountain. She found herself dreaming of how great life would be to live there where everything was possible. She just knew that in the magical kingdom her life would be easy and she could bless her family for many had told her it was enchanted with wonders abounding.

Jasmine knew the story of Cinderella because for many years her mom would read it to her before she would go to sleep. Now as she sat by the pond outside her home she thought, I am just like Cinderella. I may not have two mean stepsisters, but my life is so hard. What I really need is my prince to come and take me away from all the pain and hard work I have to do every day.

As Jasmine looked around she could see butterflies and bees finding nourishment from the spring flowers. Really, it was a lovely spring day as she sat silently contemplating her role in life. She was so happy to have such a wonderful place where she could get away. It was her quiet place that she often visited. Her secret place – yet really everyone who cared about her knew exactly where she could be found.

And today was really no different than any other day as she was thinking how much more wanted out of life. She knew, there just had to be more than just working to try to pay the bills each month. Yet, week after week and year after year she saw the difficulties of life and felt as though she were living a meager existence with no purpose.

She watched her dad go off to work each day only to come home exhausted. She had lost her mom three years earlier. Yet, it seemed like yesterday. She remembered it so well. The doctors tried to save her, but alas they could do nothing to help. Slowly, she saw her beautiful mom lose her once vibrant strength. And now, even in her grief, she was responsible to care for the home, her younger brother Theodore, the meals, and most of the outside chores. Oh, it seemed overwhelming just thinking about it.

Trying desperately to enjoy the beauty around her, she would hum and pray, only to find herself thinking again about her dilemma for she was frustrated to the point of despair. It just didn't seem fair, she pondered. Why is it that all my friends can go shopping after school, and I have to rush home?

But today, today, I can sit here by the water and dream of the possibilities. I must stop grumbling and face up to my plight. I must be a fine daughter and loyal sister for the sake of my family.

Jasmine shook her head as though trying to convince herself to snap out of her critical thinking. This is my time, she reckoned

within herself. She knew her thoughts were like a tornado, which

enviably causes damage to those in its path. And in this case it

was her life.

She was determined to overcome her circumstances and

sadness by setting her eyes and heart on something greater. But

she wasn't quite sure how to do it. So with tears flowing from

her cheeks she closed her eyes and said, "Lord, help me to just

enjoy this moment."

As she prayed this simple prayer she felt warmth in her heart.

She knew that indeed a fire still kindled there. Yes, she was alive even though the flame did not seem to satisfy her longing and grief. But she was discovering something deep within her spirit, which whispered gently to her, that it was okay to 'let go' of her responsibilities for a moment, to rest, and to dream of tomorrow.

"Yes, there must be something great ahead for me," Jasmine said out loud. "Perhaps, it is there just over the hill in the enchanted kingdom."

Jasmine was remembering the time months ago when she had seen the prince. He was handsome and so brave. She could hardly believe her eyes when she saw him fight a fierce lion and save a local farmer.

Yes, while hurrying home from school there he was just off the trail. He must have seen the lion first or maybe he was out hunting. All she knew was that he was the most handsome young man she had ever seen. Gallant and dashing just like everyone had said. Now she knew for herself. He was special! She dreamed of the day that she could see him again: the day that she could actually speak to him.

But, would that day ever come, she sighed, knowing her thoughts had taken her once again to a place, which was impossible for someone of her family background: For she was a butcher's daughter. Sure, her father did own the largest meat business in the village, but still he was a butcher and she was a butcher's daughter. And just when she was finding herself lost in a myriad of satisfying emotions she heard her brother, Theodore, calling her name.

"Jasmine, it's time to cook dinner. Dad will be home soon," he yelled.

Gosh, it couldn't be that late, she thought.

"I'm coming," she responded half-heartedly.

The time had past by so quickly, she felt. Yet, up she sprung like a swift doe for she knew it was her duty, and she never wanted to disappoint her father.

Jasmine loved her family very much and she saw the deep pain in her dad's eyes when her mom died. He didn't cry in front of her, but sometimes at night she believed she could hear sobbing from his room. Really, she was sure of it. But, she never mentioned it. She just prayed for both her father and Theodore because she knew without a doubt her younger brother whom she often called Ted was struggling.

Frequently she would find Ted crying when he thought no one was watching. And sometimes he would lash out and become angry over the littlest incidents. Like one time she had come home just a few minutes late from school because her classmate, Julie, had gotten a new musical instrument. All of her friends gathered together outside the campus talking and laughing. They all seemed so happy listening to her play it for the first time. She just wanted to be part of the group. Just for a little while, she wanted to forget and be like all the other kids who could linger around carefree as though there was nothing else of any importance.

They were having so much fun laughing, talking, and even dancing, which Jasmine loved to do almost as much as learning science. But, suddenly she realized how much time had past. She ran home, as fast as she could and there he was, a bundle of tears, crying on the steps. Theodore was so sad, and yet so mad at the same time. It was like she had done the worst possible crime. He yelled and cried for over an hour.

It took so much to calm him down and she didn't want him to tell her dad or she would really be in trouble. She pleaded with him and finally, Theodore stopped crying as she held him in her arms wiping his tears. She knew his anger was really because he was worried something had happened to her. So, she made a promise to herself and him that she would never stay after school again. And so far she hadn't broken her promise.

Theodore was always a curious boy who frequently climbed trees and once too often came home with cuts and scrapes from his mischievous behavior. He loved playing and fishing in the stream in the forest. Well, that was all before mom passed away, she thought as she was cooking. Now he stayed close to home and close to her.

Sometimes she just wanted to get away to her secret place - The place where no one bothered her and she could dream of her prince. Yet, she knew her Father and Theodore needed her. They needed her to be strong so she was determined to do her best even though her heart was broken too.

After preparing dinner, eating, doing the dishes, and her homework there was no time to really relax and watch her favorite television program. It took everything in her just to get undressed. As Jasmine slipped into bed and laid her head on the pillow she contemplated the busy days, weeks, and years ahead. She just didn't see any end to her growling life.

"Yes, this is my challenge," she whispered. "How am I going to live up to this challenge in my life? Why can't I just have a fairy godmother like Cinderella," Jasmine sobbed, "she could help me with the chores and gosh I would love a new dress. God, does anyone hear me, she cried? Does anyone care? I long to be free. Really free." She found herself yawning as she wiped her tears and in sheer exhaustion she fell fast to sleep thinking of Prince Jonathan.

Chapter 2: The Routine

The effects of the day prior didn't seem to hinder Jasmine as she leaped from her bed. It almost seemed strange to her that she would have so much energy when everything was so difficult in her life. She wondered if it could have been the prayer she prayed the night before. Maybe someone did care. Maybe someone was listening.

"Hum," she said out loud as though there was someone else in the room, "I had better get breakfast going as dad has to leave by seven and it was already six thirty."

Jasmine would have liked to be more creative, but because of time, she felt she just better get something on the table. She scrimmaged through the refrigerator and cabinets knowing her Father's taste. And finally, she decided it would just have to be pancakes again. They were always a fail safe because her dad liked them so much or at least he always ate them without complaint.

She found herself humming a simple tune her mom used to sing to her; *Just Whistle While You Work*. Funny, I am happier today, she thought. Nothing seems to be any different, yet at the some time -- something is…

Today was just like every other school day as Theodore and Jasmine rode their bikes to school, yet Jasmine felt warmth in her heart, which wasn't there for such a long time. She dropped Ted off at his school first for it was the closest, and even though it added extra time to Jasmine's day, today, she didn't seem to mind.

Now Jasmine's school was one of the top schools in the county for both their athletics and academics. Jasmine enjoyed reading and was respected by her teachers and most of her peers because she excelled in science. Truly it was her love for nature that peaked her interest.

So, she took all the science courses that she could because of her fascination of the planet and how everything worked. Outside of her chores and occasional shows, it would be accurate to say that Jasmine was fully devoted to her studies even with all her extra duties. And it wasn't a surprise to her father when she showed him her schedule containing mostly science courses as her electives.

She had finally arrived at school, just as the bell rang. Running to her first class she smiled, because she was happy to be at school. Some of her friends hated school, but she loved it. School was her time to get away from her chores, spend time with her friends, and discover new ideas. She arrived in the classroom just as the second bell rang. And as she was trying to catch her breath Anthony greeted her with a kind, "Hi."

The class was Oceanography. She hoped maybe one day she

could study dolphins, and be able to travel to all the oceans of the world. Her teacher Mister Palo was very attractive and fun to listen to which also made the subject enjoyable.

Yes, she thought, as she looked around at the other students. I'm glad this is my first class because it is challenging and everyone here wants to be here so there isn't so much distraction.

Oceanography was an advanced study elective for qualified senior students. It wasn't like the other courses where the teachers struggled just to get several of the students to participate. Really, she felt sorry for the teachers who worked so hard to make the class interesting and still some of the student just talked to each other, slept, or occasionally tried to play games on their cell phones.

Unlike them, she was in school to learn and no matter what disturbances other students brought, she was determined to do her best to achieve her goals so she could attend the State University in the fall. Besides she loved going to her elective classes, which were different because the students for the most part wanted to be there and enjoyed doing the experiments. The task today was to continue working on tide tables and tide pools.

Her science partner was also her friend, Anthony. And as always, if he was there, he was the first to greet her as she walked through the door and today was no exception.

Most of her friends said he was kind of a geek, yet it never stopped her from spending time with him. She had known Anthony all her life. Even though he wasn't the greatest athlete, or scholar for that matter - he was a 'good' friend. He was 'tried and true'. He had even rushed over to be by her side when her mom died.

She wondered sometimes what Anthony was thinking as she saw him look at her with the strangest expressions and sometimes it seemed as though he just looked right through her.

Now when she thought about it, she knew that Anthony was her best friend. Other people that she hung around with may be more popular, but it was Anthony who she trusted…if she trusted anyone. She was confident he would be there to help her if she needed him.

One would not aspire to look like Anthony, she thought, for he was average. What I mean by average is that he didn't stand out for being a great athlete, or intellectual. He was quite unassuming, not ugly, but certainly not profoundly handsome. He was, well, he was Anthony, she thought. He seemed to be fine with himself. He didn't appear to doubt or waver over every passing fad, which hit the school. Yes, look at him. He is confident, she pondered, as together – silently - they set up the tools for today's experiment.

Actually, in his geekish way -- he has a great sense of humor.

And when I am with him, I feel comfortable. With Anthony I can be myself. He assured me that it was okay to be sad at times. And above all he taught me the importance of praying and trusting God. Yes, he just seems to have an amazing confidence that many kids of our age just don't have: perhaps that is why he is my 'best friend,' Jasmine discerned to herself.

As Anthony was preparing and tinkering with the lab tools, he found himself wondering if Jasmine would ever be happy as she used to be. It seemed only rational she would be grieving given the lost of her mom and her added responsibilities.

Now she always seemed tired, but he could still see her exceptional beauty. He felt so blessed to have her as a friend for she was lovely both inside and out. He wondered if she even knew how amazing she truly was. Anthony quietly contemplated her love and kindness that she demonstrated to all, even to animals, in the midst of her ever-present anguish.

Anthony thought to himself, it is my plan to help her forget and learn to have fun even while doing to smallest things like our science experiments. Yes, he reasoned, that is my job; I will help her get her mind off all her troubles.

"Help me Lord, to think of funny things to say so I can make her smile," he prayed in his heart. Yes, there is hope. As he looked towards her, she gave him a slight smile.

"We had better get this project moving or the class is going to be over," Jasmine said, breaking the silence. As she was working and learning with Anthony she almost forgot her situation and learned to trust God.

The rest of the day just flew by as Jasmine engrossed herself in her studies. It was only during the lunch hour that she again found herself confronting her fears.

As she walked into the cafeteria she overheard a group of girls discussing the coming ball to be held at the palace. It was for the prince's birthday and he was to choose his bride. There was such a great buzz going on in the room as many of the girls talked about what they would wear and whether they would get an invitation. There was even chatter regarding the stories of how the kingdom was enchanted and the miracles that took place there. How could it be that a place so close to her home could offer so many mysteries? So many dreams filled her head…

As a butcher's daughter, she doubted there would be an invitation for her. And besides, even if she got one, she would have difficulty finding an appropriate dress for such an occasion. She dismissed the thought with a tinge of sadness, as she felt her prince was far removed from her.

The day forged on and there was a furious sense of hopelessness wailing up inside of her. The joy she felt early in the morning was now replaced with dread. Once again she allowed her mind to focus on the impossibility of change in her future as revolving thoughts of despair and disappointment spiraled clouding her thinking. Yet, in her innermost being she decided to call out once again to the Lord for help.

 "God," she prayed, "I want to go the ball. I want to wear a beautiful dress, and I want the prince to see me. Is it even possible, Lord, that such a gallant prince, could see me?"

Yet, in her innermost being she decided to call out once again to the Lord for help!

Chapter 3: The Invitation

Her future looked uncertain and dim with regards to going to the ball, yet the warmth of the sunshine beaming down through the trees, as she rode home, gave Jasmine a sense of peace. She was determined to break the revolving thoughts of sadness that plagued her.

"I will face my challenges," Jasmine whispered to herself.

"There are so many things that I have in my life to be thankful for."

She was remembering something Anthony had shared with her one day as he was reading his Bible. He said, "You know, people should give thanks even when things are difficult." Actually, he is pretty good at following true to that, she reckoned.

So, I guess I should at least try and find things to be thankful for, she thought. Yes, I am grateful for my dad and for my brother, even though sometimes he is a pain. And, I am thankful I have a home to live in, as some people don't.

Yet, the news of the coming ball kept creeping into her thoughts, like a spider onto a web. How can I give thanks for that? How can I be thankful that others are more fortunate than me? Yet, I must try. I must try to give thanks even when things don't go my way.

Quietly, Jasmine began to sing a sweet song she had heard her mother sing several times. *"Give thanks with a grateful heart. Give thanks to the Holy One. Give thanks because He's given Jesus Christ His Son. Give thanks."*

She always liked the song and found singing always made her feel better. She was almost home now and needed to concentrate on the tasks at hand. Ted would be home and she would need to get him on his homework, prepare him a snack, as well as start dinner all while she was trying to do her own studies.

Time seemed to slip by. As the clock struck six she realized her dad was late again. Dinner was almost ready, but she still had a lot of homework to finish. She put all the pots on simmer as she studied for her history examination, which was fourth period. She wasn't too worried, as she knew she could also study during lunch break, which was a relief since she also had a book report to finish for her literature class.

Ted has it easy she thought - just a little math and reading then he gets to play. She heard a car pull into the driveway and knew it was her dad. So, she walked over to the stove to stir the stew she had prepared for dinner.

She greeted her Father at the door and he gave her a big hug. There was a smirk on his face and she knew something was up.

"Dad" she said, almost teasing him. "What's going on?"

He put his hand in his pocket and pulled out a white envelope with a golden seal on it. She thought to herself as quickly as she heard herself say it.

"It couldn't be an invitation to Prince Jonathan's ball. How could I be invited?"

Her dad smiled as he explained how he had been asked to supply the meat for the event. The kingdom's Chief of Staff was so happy with the price he had given them. Therefore, they asked if he knew anyone who would like to attend the ball. He said yes, and they presented him with an invitation.

"Wow, but how can I go, Dad," Jasmine said reluctantly.

"I don't have a dress, and I would just look like a fool in front of the other guests."

"I don't even know how to dance well. Oh dad, I can't go, but it is awesome I was given an invitation," she said holding back the tears.

"Sure you can honey," her dad replied. "We can get a dress. I have saved up a little money."

But she knew the money he was speaking of was their savings for a new car, which they were in great need of. Their old Ford truck had over 200,000 miles on it. Truly, it was a wonder it still ran at all.

She thought of all the sacrifices her dad had made for her and Ted since her mom died. All he really ever did now was work, but she also knew it was his choice in hoping that by staying busy he wouldn't think so much. And here he was persuading Jasmine to go to the ball and use the money he had saved for their new car.

Yes, indeed she had much to be thankful for. She hugged her Father tightly. "Oh, dad, you make me so happy. There is no way I will use the money for the car, but you're truly the best dad in the world!"

That night as she went to bed she pondered on the truth of just how blessed she was to have such a loving father. She felt the warmth in her heart continue to grow. Sure she was disappointed, but she declared, "I will not be shallow in my thoughts Lord. I choose to be grateful and give thanks for all things just as Anthony taught me."

She began to believe that God does make a way where there seems to be no way. Jasmine shared with the Lord, "I am going to be a better daughter. I am going to be thankful when things are difficult. I may not have a fairy godmother like Cinderella, but I have a dad who wants the very best for me."

She found herself reading the invitation over and over again mused with the unlikely becoming plausible. She would smile, laugh and then cry. Yes, once again she was dreaming of the enchanted kingdom and Price Jonathon who was just over the hill. It seemed just too far from her reach. As she gazed out her window she could almost see the lights faintly in the distance. Yet, it might as well be a continent away. It was merely a dream; she rationalized to herself closing her eyes with hope in her heart for a new day.

*She began to believe that God does make
a way where there seems to be no way.*

Chapter 4: The Expectation

Weeks had pasted by and summer was approaching. Along with her friends, everyone was busy studying for finals, discovering which college they would attend in the fall, and of course getting ready for the ball. That is if they were fortunate enough to have gotten an invitation. Jasmine's invitation sat next to her bed. It was worn and crumpled from all the times she had read it imagining the events of the evening.

She had reduced her thinking to that which was rational as she was a logical girl determined to handle her plight with dignity. And no matter how much it hurt inside she was not going to express her thoughts with Julie or the other girls at school for that matter. Only Anthony seemed to understand her unspoken words.

She was determined not to divulge the fact she had been given an invitation because she felt it would be bragging. Besides, she wasn't going anyway so why not join in with those who couldn't attend so they wouldn't feel alone and rejected.

When she was around her friends who were so excited they were going and who discussed all their plans for the event, she tried hard to act pleased for them despite her true feelings. Really in her heart she was a bit envious.

Now she put her attention towards Ted who appeared to be doing better these days, too. She believed it was probably because he was so happy school would be finished in a few short weeks. There were even a couple of days where she was a few minutes late from school, and he didn't get too upset. She found him just playing in the yard by the pond. This made her happy because she could see he was healing.

Jasmine's father's routine was also pretty much the same. Although, he was late most nights about six-thirty or seven rather than six so Jasmine was used to fixing dinners, which could be easily warmed up.

Just as she had done for the past three years – she was

preparing dinner when the bell rang. It was about 6:30 and her father was late again. She thought it was strange someone would come by during the dinner hour. But, she turned the burners down and quickly ran to the door. When she opened the door there was a man with a special delivery for her. A package! She knew at once it was a gown. Wow, her dad had gone ahead and bought her a gown for the ball, she thought.

She signed for the package and placed it on the table as she waited for her father to come home.

"Dad, where are you," she said quietly to herself.

Ted was watching television and she found herself shaking the package wanting to open it, but knowing she should wait for her father. She was growing more anxious by the moment. Where could her dad be, she wondered? And finally at a half pasted seven she heard his truck drove up.

Eagerly she ran to the door.

"Dad, what did you do?" she exclaimed. But, her dad looked puzzled for a moment and then said, "Yes, I am quite late. I'm sorry for not calling."

"No dad, I'm talking about the package. You sent the package? Come and see for yourself," exclaimed Jasmine as she grabbed hold of his arm directing him to the table where it laid.

Jasmine opened the package and inside was the most beautiful pink gown she had ever seen. She began to cry. Hugging her dad and brother while jumping up and down in pure delight, she held it up to herself. She looked in the mirror on the wall and danced throughout the room. But, her dad seemed just as surprised as she was with the dress.

He didn't say anything for a few minutes and just let her dance as he admired her - For he had not seen her so happy in years. Finally, he told her. "Honey, my precious Jasmine. It was not me who bought the dress."

"Then who could have it been dad," Jasmine said still holding the dress up with a smile on her face.

"I'm not sure, but I will do some checking as it must be someone who wants to see you go to the ball," he said.

"Wow, they spent a pretty penny on this gown. It has been imported from the next county. Yes, what fine craftsmanship," he marveled looking at and dress and wondering who could have given this tremendous gift to his daughter.

"So I guess you are going to the ball after all my dear. Surely God has heard your prayers. Now there is nothing to stop you except yourself. So wipe those tears from your eyes and let's eat our dinner as we discuss your plans," he said with a smile.

Dinner was magnificent that night for even Ted was full of joy over the excitement of his sister going to the ball. It was only a week away, and he knew that she would be especially happy everyday. Ted marveled at his father's love for them and newfound energy to celebrate with Jasmine at such a late hour with work in the morning.

Jasmine could hardly contain her excitement throughout the week. But still she had decided to keep it a secret that she was attending the ball just in case something happened to squash her plans. Perhaps it is a mistake, she rationalized within her mind, and someone will come and get the dress saying it was not intended for her after all.

In first period, Anthony was already getting their next science project off the ground. He had been staying after school preparing for finals and especially giving extra attention to their last science project as it reflected a good part of their overall grade. She was grateful for his help because she knew if it hadn't been for his continued encouragement and help she would have never made it through this course or really school for that matter. Part of her wanted to share with Anthony about the ball because he was always so good to her, but she was resolute in her decision for secrecy.

From first to last period - the day just seemed to fly by. Everything seemed easy today. The entire school was talking about the ball, and there was expectancy in the air.

Wow! Jasmine said quietly to herself, even though I have all my chores to do today, it just doesn't matter because I am going to the ball. "I am going to the ball. Ha ha… I am going to the ball," Jasmine sang softly as she quickly rode her bike home. Everything seemed lovelier today.

"Could it be…could it be that the God has heard all my prayers? Could He love me this much that He has made a way where there seemed to be no way? Yes, it is I. Lord, Jasmine! I am going to the ball tonight and nothing can stop me," she giggled. "You are for me and nothing can come against me!" She sang with delight, "And I have a great future and a hope."

These are the very words she had heard Anthony speak so

many times when they hung out together, and her mom shared these same words with her several times, but they never seemed to mean much. Today they did. Today, she dreamed almost anything could be possible as she sang these words she knew there was a new song in her heart.

Even though it felt like butterflies in her stomach, she chuckled to herself. I wonder what the prince will wear. And I wonder if he will even notice me. "Everyone will look beautiful," she remarked to herself. "Wow! It is going to be the 'best' night ever. I am going to the ball! It is amazing… I am going to the ball at the enchanted kingdom," she shouted out loud once she made sure there was no one around who could hear her. "Yes, I am going to a ball at the enchanted kingdom and may be, just may

be, I am going to meet the prince," she proclaimed.

"You are for me and nothing can come
against me!"

Chapter 5: The Ball

Visions of precious images filled Jasmine's mind as she prepared for the event of the season. She twirled around the room, glimpsing in the mirror from time to time as she caught her reflection. Then she boldly walked to the full-length mirror and said out loud these very words.

She said, "I am not just a butcher's daughter, but I am the daughter of the King of Kings and Lord of Lords. I am important and I have value. No, I don't have a magic chariot to pick me up like Cinderella did, but my amazing dad is having one of his friends deliver me in style in his brand new silver BMW. So, even if I don't meet the prince I am still getting to ride in a

BMW for the first time; I am wearing the most beautiful dress I have ever had, and I am going to the enchanted kingdom to the ball," she declared with grace and excitement.

After touching up her makeup one final time she whisked down the stairs, but before she could reach the bottom she heard her father say, "stop!" She stopped in her tacks. Her father looked up to her and spoke gently, "Honey you are beautiful. I am so proud of you!"

She knew in her heart that his words were tender and sincere, but replied, "Daddy, stop it you are going to make me cry and then I will mess up my makeup."

Yet, his words truly touched her deeply for he hadn't said anything like that since her mom died. They just seemed to be going through the motions of life. Today…tonight…was different. She knew this night might be the most important night in her life.

Her dad's friend arrived sharply at 6:30 as planned and he graciously opened the door for her as she got into the back seat. She could smell the new leather seats and was so happy it wasn't just her imagination. She knew it was real. Now she found herself thinking of all the times she reflected by the pond – her secret place – where she would pray and dream, hoping for this day. And now the day was here.

She was on her way to the magical kingdom with her tattered invitation in her hand. The impossible became reality. But, still as happy as she was, she wondered, just what the night would be like.

Now they were entering into the enchanted forest and really it looked pretty much like any other forest she had seen. Granted the trees seemed a bit larger and you could hear the wind rustling through the leaves. Some of the trees seemed to sway with the rhythm of her heart.

"I wonder if this forest is alive and knows my thoughts." Jasmine marveled at the beauty around her. She rolled down the window to listen carefully. The warm air felt invigorating and only heightened her enthusiasm. She looked for birds, deer, or any form of wildlife. But, only saw a few squirrels scurrying up the trees. Then with the blink of her eyes she saw something remarkable. There was a body of water. It seemed to be flowing forth from what looked like a thrown. And around the water were people dancing.

There were birds, and several kinds of animals, deer, antelope, and even a bear, yet the people didn't seem to be concerned. Her father's friend slowed down the car so they could get a better look. Yes, it was magical.

"I am certain this is why it is called the enchanted kingdom because animals and people seem to be in harmony. Gosh – if this is the forest, just think what the castle must be like," Jasmine exclaimed to her father's friend.

Her heart was pounding so strong that she could feel it. There – up ahead - less than one hundred meters before them was a mesmerizing castle. Captured by its beauty from the meticulous grounds to the spiral stairways leading to enormous golden doors she found herself in awe.

Jasmine knew it was going to take all her strength to get the nerve to enter in. But, she was going. She looked down trembling at her hand, which was holding her shabby invitation, and said, "I can do all things, with Christ who strengths me."   Her faith was growing as she took her foot from the car and with every step she took moving forward she noticed she was no longer trembling. There was no turning back. Nor was there any desire to retreat. The past was behind her. Now she trusted God fully – believing - a new day was dawning on her life.

As she moved up the staircase there was ease in her step - an assurance that this evening was paramount to her future. As she reached the top of the stairway, the doors opened automatically as though they had sensed her presence. In fact, she was aware of a sweet presence around her.

She couldn't see it with her eyes, but she knew she was not alone as she climbed the steps. There was an invisible force around her. This force actually helped to strengthen her as she climbed the steps. It was warm and inviting. She felt a calm or perhaps peace. It was difficult for her to fully comprehend, as it was a new experience. This presence gave her greater peace and joy than she had felt in her lifetime.

When she entered the room there was a hush for only a moment. Then there was laughter and joy beyond words. The exquisite craftsmanship of the palace took second place to the mere beauty of the lovely people in the room. Everyone is beautiful, Jasmine thought. It is amazing! Everyone is special! Her eyes were full of tears of joy as she looked around the ballroom.

Some people were eating; some were dancing, and others were

having conversations. There was a greater love and joy in her heart that she had never felt before. The pain of her mom's death seemed to disappear. She had gotten so accustomed to that pain. Now it was gone and in its place there seemed to be greater warmth in her heart as it was set aflame.

Yes, it was like someone had lit a fire in her heart. She stood at the entrance wanting to fully enter in, but at the same time she was fearful of the fire in her heart, which seemed to consume her. There was a burning love and passion for everyone. She began to laugh and cry at the same time.

And to her surprise there were several people she knew from her village. Her friend Julie was on the balcony playing her flute along with an enormous orchestra with people of all different nationalities. And yes, Anthony was there too. He looked so handsome in his suit.

"Funny, he never even mentioned that he was coming to the ball," she chuckled, "but neither did I."

"So I have come this far," Jasmine, said quietly under her breath. "Lord, help me to go all the way. For I long to meet Prince Jonathan." And just as she whispered those words, Jonathan stepped beside her.

As he reached out his hand she took it and together they moved forth as though dancing on water. There was music and harmony and Jasmine felt as though she and the prince were the only ones in the room.

Not a word was spoken for his eyes said it all as he lovingly looked into my soul. Jasmine realized this love was pure. It was holy and sacrificing. She knew in that moment she was loved, truly loved by the 'prince of peace.'

The fire that consumed her heart was one, which would be lasting. They danced with elegance and ease as revelation sprang into her being giving her new hope for the future. As the music came to a close she was not sad but satisfied knowing there was much more to come.

Jasmine looked at the prince and wanted so badly to say, 'who have you chosen as your wife?' She knew that the whole purpose of the ball was for him to find his bride.

As the clock began to chime she realized she must get back to the car or she would miss her ride so off she ran, but not without losing one of her slippers.

All the way home she continued to feel the warmth of the love from the prince in her heart. She felt a sweet force not only around her, but also in her very being. It was tangible and she realized that though it might not seem rational because it couldn't be seen, her faith and desire to believe truly was the most logical thing she had ever done because it was healing. It was God! And her only prayer that night was, "Thank you Lord! May I always know you as I know you now for I realize that I have never known your love until tonight."

The consuming fire that burned

in her soul was in fact real.

Chapter 6: The Slipper

Dreams filled Jasmine's heart as she slept. She wasn't really sure how to even explain the events of the evening to her father and brother. And what of Anthony, he was there too. Surly Anthony would have lots of questions for he must have seen her dance with Prince Jonathan.

She gave thanks to God for the night before as she looked over at her dress remembering the evening. She touched her heart, which was full of passion and love for the prince. There was no pain remaining, for miraculously it had been healed and replaced with a fiery love of God.

Happily, she pulled her jeans on and found a cute tee shirt to wear. Humming as she brushed her teeth. She knew her life was changed. Yes, she was transformed. She had danced with the prince, and she knew he loved her even though they didn't exchange words.

As she walked down stairs she saw her father sitting at the kitchen table just as she imagined he would be. Waiting… He was eagerly waiting to hear the events of the night. So Jasmine, full of love, hugged her father and sat down to tell him all about her evening and the events which took place with the prince.

She told him about the enchanted forest; about the joy, and the laughter; about the beauty of the people from every tribe, every tongue, and every nation. She shared about her friends who were there, and that really everyone who wanted to be at the palace was given an invitation.

She told him they didn't even ask for an invitation, but it was the people who felt they needed one to get in. She shared the love she felt in her heart and the fire that burned even now. She even shared that in her hurry to get home she had lost her slipper.

Her father listened intently as tears fell down his cheeks. He could see and feel the change in his daughter. He saw a light in her eyes and a glow in her spirit.

He spoke gently to her, "Oh honey, I too would like to meet the prince. I long to feel the love you have experienced."

Just as her father spoke those words there was a knock on the door. Brushing back the tears, Jasmine's father walked to the door and opened it to see Prince Jonathan standing on their porch with love in his eyes.

Chapter 7: The Discovery

And once again Prince Jonathan's hand was extended, but this time it was not to dance. In his hand he held Jasmine's slipper. He greeted Jasmine's father as he waited for an invitation to enter into their home.

"Hello Prince Jonathan I have been excited to meet you! Please come in," replied Jasmine's father. The prince began to tell Jasmine's father how lovely his daughter was. He said, "Jasmine is a precious flower and her fragrance is a delight for me. Last night as she left, she hastened so quickly; she dropped her slipper. I wanted to personally make sure she got it back right away for it is an important part of her armor. She is so lovely and her slippers will help her to do the work of the Gospel."

"What do you mean?" Jasmine's father asked. "In the enchanted kingdom my bride wears armor and the shoes are essential for as my bride she will bring forth the Gospel of peace. The Gospel is the story of my 'goodness'. And the truth is that I am alive and desire to have relationship with the people in this world.

Yes, I have clothed Jasmine and prepared her for this time. The dress I sent to your daughter was pink because I knew she would love it. The color pink represents healthy flesh. You see she is fully whole in me. I combined the red from my blood (my sacrifice), which was shed, and the white, which symbolizes purity and holiness to bring forth pink - healthy flesh. She is my bride, and she is fully healthy in me.

My name is Jonathan which is a nick name given to me by some in the Kingdom. It means God gives. You see my Father has given me to this world so that people will find hope, love, and forgiveness. My Father and I desire for people to bring the enchanted kingdom 'to earth as it is in heaven' so my bride will live in freedom and authority.

I desire for 'my bride' to be released from the pain and fear in their lives, which holds them back from achieving their full destiny. My bride will be without spot or wrinkle because I clothe them in my righteousness. I not only clothe them, but I give them a crown and scepter of authority in which to live on this earth with as they remain in my presence releasing my fruit to others.

Jasmine has been seeking me for a long time, and I have always been close to her. It wasn't until she entered the enchanted kingdom and encountered me that her eyes where fully opened. But, I was always there watching her and sending my angles to protect her. My mercy covered her and you during the difficulties you faced with your wife's passing. You see, I love you and it grieved me to see your pain even though your wife is at peace with me.

But, truly the greatest news is you too can be part of my

kingdom. You too can be my bride. When I heard you say you wanted to encounter my love I knocked on your door. I knew you were ready for I have been pursuing you.

Your daughter Jasmine paved the way. She was willing to face her fears and step forward in faith seeking me. As Jasmine visited me in the enchanted kingdom she saw the love of God and the gift that was always hers. In my kingdom anything is possible for those who believe. So, I am celebrating with the Father, Holy Spirit, and angles todays as you invited me in.

Chapter 8: The Beginning

Truly, today was the beginning of a magical life of the possibilities to be unfolded in the days and years ahead. Jasmine realized, though she dreamed of being Cinderella for so long in actuality her life was so much better than that of Cinderella's. For the story of Cinderella - as beautiful as it was - was still only an elaborate fairy tale.

Yet, in real life Jasmine now discovered hope beyond her pain and fear. She knew that by accepting this gift of love from God her life would never be the same.

No longer was she to spend her days and nights filled with

regret in the ashes of despair, but instead her heart was on fire with a passion for her savior. She knew there was still much work to be done, but she would never be alone. As the prince's bride she had a purpose beyond herself, which gave her the strength to get up out of the ashes and faith to hold onto the truth of God's love.

Jasmine reflected on the words of her prince who assured her that his presence was always near. He even told her there was a purpose in everything in her life to include the vehicle she arrived in. It was a BMW because he was calling her forth to be his warrior (Be My Warrior). Never would she let the fire go out that burned in her heart.

She was determined to wear her slippers and spread the goodness of the enchanted kingdom to everyone wherever she would go. For the Prince had shared with her that as a bride she was a carrier of the kingdom. Yes, God's presence was in her and with her now as she walked forth in her journey. She had greater confidence and vitality because of the revelation that she was growing with him. She was happy to tell the people of the marvelous power and love she had experienced.

Rejoicing, Jasmine was eager to share with others her new life, which she had been given. It was as though she was awakened from a bad dream. She was sure of her position in the royal family and felt peace for the first time regarding her mom's death. She didn't blame God, but knew her mom was safe with God the Father. Jasmine now realized, everyone has been given an invitation. All they have to do is open it up, and believe in the 'prince of peace' to enter in.

Also, she now understood she was more than blessed because the prince had visited her home. Her father had asked him in. She smiled because she was certain his heart too would be changed. As she sat by the pond and looked out the Enchanted Kingdom she wondered at how close it had always been. Just how close the prince had been.

She pondered at the love of God to give her his son, and such great friends. And of course the Holy Spirit whom Prince

Jonathan promised would teach her all things. He would lead her and guide her in her life's journey. She was so happy for she realized that she was no longer hopeless and miserable. Her old nature was gone and she was reborn on that precious night when she encountered the prince. Yet, she also realized for the first time, even when she felt weak and vulnerable in her past, he was there.

It was so amazing because he even sent his angles to help her, and would continue to do so throughout her life. Now she could see so clearly. Now she could see he was there, in her life, all along.

For a moment she looked into the field watching her brother

play and contemplated when he too would come to know the prince. For now she realized it was part of her destiny to share about who the Prince was with others. And she knew it would be easy and fun because she was amazed by his love and goodness. Her heart, no longer ached, but was filled with great joy. She began to laugh, dance, and swirl rejoicing in triumph.

Lost in celebration she heard a familiar voice. It was the voice of Anthony. Anthony: her best friend. He never gave up on her and always prayed for her. Suddenly, Jasmine realized just how blessed she was to have Anthony in her life.

"Jasmine, where are you? Jasmine!" she heard him calling as he came closer for he always knew just where to find her. Jasmine jumped up and ran towards Anthony, declaring with tears of joy, "I know him! I really know him!" She grabbed hold of Anthony hugging him tightly.

Anthony simply hugged her back while patting her lightly declaring in his soft confident manner, "I know. I know."

Jasmine still hugging Anthony exclaimed with glee, "A new day had dawned and surly this is just the beginning…

Characters Names & Meanings

1. **Anthony**: Worthy of praise, highly praiseworthy, and he is priceless

2. **Cinderella**: Girl of the cinders and of the ashes. It is French, English, and Latin American.

3. **Jasmine:** Strong Fragrant Flower, and Messenger of Love.

4. **Jonathan:** A common masculine given **name meaning** "YHWH has given" in Hebrew

5. **Julie:** A popular French first name which originally comes from the Latin Julia which could **mean** youthful, soft-haired, beautiful or vivacious. It is the feminine

6. **Theodore:** An English masculine given **name**. It comes from the Greek **name** Θεόδωρος (Theōdoros) **meaning** "God's gift".

Just like Jasmine, Jesus Christ wants to burn brightly in your heart bringing you great joy and fulfillment in your life. You can and will have victory with Him!

Zetaxcentaur

Pianeti extrasolari disegni da colorare

Fiordelisi Massimiliano

Zetaxcentaur

Pianeti extrasolari disegni da colorare

Dovete colorare la figura in bianco e nero come la

figura d'esempio a colori.